Karen Kramer is lost in the airport!

"It's time to find my friend," Mr. Jansen said. "He told me that flying makes him hungry. He said he would wait for us in one of the snack places."

"There's a snack place," Eric said, and pointed. "It's called The Pita Palace."

"There's another one," Cam said, "Polly's Ice Cream."

Mr. Jansen said, "There are lots of snack shops here. There's Sol's Sandwiches, Fresh Squeezed Juice, Happy Burgers, and lots more. We don't have to look in every shop for Max. I'll just call him on his cell phone. He'll tell me where he is."

Mr. Jansen took his cell phone from his pocket.

"Karen! Karen Kramer!" someone shouted. "Karen Kramer, where are you?"

Cam, Eric, and Mr. Jansen turned.

"Have you seen her?" asked a man standing nearby. "Have you seen my daughter Karen? She's just five years old, and she's lost."

CAM JANSEN

CASE #33

and the Spaghetti Max Mystery

For MacKenzie,
David A Adler

David A. Adler

illustrated by Joy Allen

School #4

Gold Award Library

PUFFIN BOOKS
An Imprint of Penguin Group (USA)

PUFFIN BOOKS
An imprint of Penguin Young Readers Group
Published by the Penguin Group
Penguin Group (USA) Inc.
375 Hudson Street
New York, New York 10014, U.S.A.

USA * Canada * UK * Ireland * Australia
New Zealand * India * South Africa * China

penguin.com
A Penguin Random House Company

First published in the United States of America by Viking,
an imprint of Penguin Young Readers Group, 2013
Published by Puffin Books, an imprint of Penguin Young Readers Group, 2014

THE LIBRARY OF CONGRESS HAS CATALOGED THE VIKING EDITION AS FOLLOWS:
Adler, David A.
Cam Jansen and the Spaghetti Max mystery / by David A. Adler ; illustrated by Joy Allen.
pages cm
Summary: While at the airport waiting for her father to pick up his best friend from childhood,
Cam Jansen uses her photographic memory to help a distressed father find his missing daughter.
ISBN 978-0-670-01260-2 (hardcover)
[1. Mystery and detective stories. 2. Memory—Fiction. 3. Airports—Fiction.
4. Missing children—Fiction.] I. Allen, Joy, illustrator. II. Title.
PZ7.A2615Calqf 2013 [Fic]—dc23 2012044877

Puffin Books ISBN 978-0-14-751232-1

Printed in the United States of America

5 7 9 10 8 6 4

For my grandson Jacob,

Happy reading!

—D.A.A.

To Spaghetti Bev, and Papa Giani's!

—J.A.

CAM JANSEN

and the
Spaghetti Max
Mystery

Chapter One

"Spaghetti Max," Mr. Jansen said as he got out of his car. "Spaghetti Max."

Cam Jansen and her best friend, Eric Shelton, got out of the car, too. They were in a parking lot at the airport. They all walked toward the large building just ahead.

"Spaghetti Max," Mr. Jansen said again. "I can't believe it. Spaghetti Max."

"Why do you keep saying that?" Cam Jansen asked her father.

"I'm so excited to see Max. He was my best friend when I was in grade school. We did everything together."

"Like Eric and I do," Cam said.

"Yes, like you and Eric. Then, just before we started sixth grade, his family moved. I haven't seen him since then."

"Wow!" Eric said. "That's a really long time."

"It's been almost thirty years. But we got back in touch recently on the internet. And now he's coming to town for a few days, and he's staying with us."

"Dad," Cam said. "Tell Eric why you call him Spaghetti Max."

"His real name is Max Miller. But he's really skinny, like a strand of spaghetti. So we gave him the nickname 'Spaghetti Max.' He called me 'Barry J.' The J is for Jansen."

"I know about nicknames," Eric said. "'Cam' is a nickname. Her real name is Jennifer."

Cam is short for "the Camera." She's called that because of her amazing memory. It's like she has a camera in her head with pictures in there of everything she's seen.

"I want a nickname, too," Eric said. "You could call me Spaghetti Eric."

Cam looked at her friend.

"You're not so skinny," she said.

"Then call me Ziti Eric. Ziti is a big noodle."

Cam, Eric, and Cam's father had reached the airport departure and arrivals building.

"Or call me Pizza Eric. I like pizza. Or call me Scooter Shelton, because I run so fast."

Mr. Jansen turned and looked at the hundreds of cars in the parking lot. "With all this talk about noodles and scooters, I forgot

to look where I parked my car. How will I find it later?"

Cam closed her eyes. She said, *"Click!"* Cam always says *"Click!"* when she wants to remember something. She says it's the sound her mental camera makes.

"I'm looking at a picture I have in my head," Cam said. "Your car is parked between a red sports car and a silver SUV. It's in section B4."

Cam opened her eyes.

"B4," Eric said. "That's easy. It's the word *before*. Even I can remember that."

Cam, Eric, and Cam's father turned and went into the airport building. It was a busy place.

People pulling suitcases on wheels were hurrying to the departure gates.

People stood looking up at a large computer screen. On the screen was the schedule of arriving and departing airplanes.

There was a long line of people standing by the information desk.

The building was also a noisy place. There were lots of announcements.

*Flight four seventy-eight from New York
now arriving at gate eleven.
Flight ninety-three to New Orleans now
boarding at gate sixteen.*

"I made a big WELCOME SPAGHETTI MAX!!
sign," Cam told Eric. "I taped it to the front
door of our house."

"It's time to find my friend," Mr. Jansen
said. "He told me that flying makes him

hungry. He said he would wait for us in one of the snack places."

"There's a snack place," Eric said, and pointed. "It's called The Pita Palace."

"There's another one," Cam said, "Polly's Ice Cream."

Mr. Jansen said, "There are lots of snack shops here. There's Sol's Sandwiches, Fresh Squeezed Juice, Happy Burgers, and lots more. We don't have to look in every shop for Max. I'll just call him on his cell phone. He'll tell me where he is."

Mr. Jansen took his cell phone from his pocket.

"Karen! Karen Kramer!" someone shouted. "Karen Kramer, where are you?"

Cam, Eric, and Mr. Jansen turned.

"Have you seen her?" asked a man standing nearby. "Have you seen my daughter Karen? She's just five years old, and she's lost."

Chapter Two

"I'm Mel Kramer," the man said. "And I'm worried."

"This is my friend Cam," Eric told Mr. Kramer. "She has a great memory. She'll remember if she saw your daughter."

Mr. Jansen said, "Cam is also great at solving mysteries."

"Did you see her?" the man asked Cam. "Did you see Karen?"

"What does she look like?" Cam asked.

Mel Kramer held his hand at the height of Cam's shoulders.

"She's about this tall," he said. "She has

strawberry red ribbons in her hair." He smiled and said, "She's so cute."

Mr. Jansen asked, "What is she wearing?"

Mr. Kramer thought for a moment.

"An avocado green shirt and a banana yellow belt."

"Strawberries! Avocados! Bananas! " Eric whispered. "That's a wacky salad but it's making me hungry."

Cam closed her eyes. She said, *"Click!"*

She said, *"Click!"* again.

"Cam has a photographic memory," Eric told Mr. Kramer. "It's like she has pictures

in her head of every-
thing she's seen. Now
she's looking at pic-
tures of people she's
seen at the airport.
Maybe one of them
is Karen."

Cam opened her
eyes.

"I'm sorry," she
said. "I didn't see
her."

"She was right over there," Mel Kramer
said. He pointed toward the men's bathroom.
"I told her I was going in for just a minute. I
told her to wait for me."

Cam, Eric, and Mr. Jansen looked where
the man had pointed. There was a large sign
on the door that said MEN.

"I was going into the bathroom, but she
thought it was a restaurant."

"It says MEN on the door," Eric said. "Why
did she think that's a restaurant?"

"She saw MEN and thought it said MENU," Mr. Kramer explained.

"When Cam was five, she did the same thing," Mr. Jansen said. "She was just learning to read. She saw the first few letters of something and thought she knew the whole word. Once she saw a sign that said TOY STORE and she thought it said TOE STORE."

"I remember that," Cam said. "I wanted to go and look at all the toes!"

Mel Kramer turned, looked at the door to the men's room, and said, "I was only in there for a minute or two, and now she's gone."

"It only takes a minute for someone to get lost," Mr. Jansen told him.

There was another announcement:

Flight sixty-three for Los Angeles now boarding at gate twenty-three.

"I help Cam solve mysteries," Eric told Mr. Kramer. "We may be able to find your daughter."

Eric pointed to the toy shop near the men's room.

"Karen could have gone in there."

They all walked to the store. There was a small table in front. On it were several battery-powered animals walking and bumping into each other.

"Look at that monkey," Eric said. "*Bam!* It just crashed into the giraffe. And—*bam!*—

the elephant crashed into the lion. These crashing toys are fun!"

Mr. Jansen said, "Karen loves stuffed animals. Maybe she saw the crashing animals in the front and went inside to find the stuffed animals."

It was a small store with toys, games, and books for children. Lots of parents and their children were looking at the toys. Cam, Eric, Mr. Jansen, and Mr. Kramer walked through the store. They found the stuffed animals, but they didn't find Karen Kramer.

"She knows not to wander off," her father said. "We've been in this airport lots of times. This is the first time she's gotten lost."

Mr. Jansen said, "Maybe she went with someone to the gate where your airplane is boarding."

"She knows not to go off with a stranger. I've taught her that—don't talk to strangers, and if you need help, find the police. But maybe she went by herself to the gate."

Mr. Kramer's hands shook as he took two long slips of paper from his pocket.

"These are our boarding passes," he said softly. "Karen knows we are supposed to leave from gate eighteen."

He looked at the signs against the wall.

"Gate eighteen is that way," he said, and pointed to the right. He started toward the gate. Then he stopped. "To get to the gate you need to pass through the security check. And to pass through security, you need a boarding pass. She doesn't have one. I have it."

Eric leaned close to Cam and whispered, "He's about to cry."

"I'm worried," Mr. Kramer said. "This is the first time she's gotten lost."

"Don't worry," Eric told Mr. Kramer. "We'll find your daughter."

Chapter Three

"Maybe we shouldn't look for your daughter," Cam's father said.

"What?" Mr. Kramer said, raising his voice. "I can't just leave her here."

"I said that wrong. What I meant is that we should let her know where you are. We should go to the information desk and ask them to make an announcement."

"I know where the information desk is," Cam said. "We passed it on our way in."

They all followed Cam through the busy airport building.

"While we walk," Mr. Kramer said, "keep

looking for Karen. Remember, she is wearing an avocado green shirt."

"I remember," Eric whispered. "Avocados, bananas, and strawberries."

There was another announcement:

> *Flight one nineteen for Houston now boarding at gate eleven.*

There was a long line of people waiting by the information desk. Mr. Kramer got on the end of the line. It was moving slowly.

"You stay here," Mr. Jansen told him. "I'll go to one of the ticket windows. Maybe they can make the announcement."

Eric said, "We'll look for her. We're kids, just like Karen. Maybe we can figure out where she is."

Cam, Eric, and Mr. Jansen walked away from the line.

"You have to promise me you'll stay together," Mr. Jansen told Cam and Eric. "I don't want you to get lost, too."

"We promise," Cam and Eric said.

Mr. Jansen walked toward the ticket windows. There were lines there, too.

"What's your idea?" Cam asked Eric. "Where do you think Karen is?"

Eric turned a little and looked. He turned a little more and looked some more. When he had turned all the way around, he told Cam, "I have no idea where she is. I just thought we are better at finding people and solving mysteries when it's just the two of us."

"Let's go to the last place her dad saw her," Cam said. "Let's go to the men's room."

Cam and Eric stood just outside the men's room. Men hurried into it. Some were pulling suitcases on wheels. And men hurried out.

"Yuck!" Cam whispered. "Each time that door opens I smell bathroom."

"Bathroom?"

"You know, that ammonia cleaner smell."

The door opened again. A man holding onto a small boy's hand came out. "Next time," the man told the boy, "don't wait until the last minute to tell me you have to go."

"Did you smell it?" Cam asked.

"Yeah," Eric said, and pinched his nose closed.

"Do you know how that makes me feel?" Cam asked.

Eric shook his head. He didn't know.

"It makes me feel like *I* have to go to the bathroom."

Cam looked around. To the left of the men's room was the toy shop. To the right of the men's room was the women's room.

"Maybe that's it," Cam said. "Maybe Karen stood here waiting for her father. Then suddenly she felt she had to go, so what did she do?"

Eric shook his head again.

Cam laughed.

"When you have to go, you have to go," Cam said. "So she went to the bathroom."

"You have to go, too," Eric said. "You have to go in there and look for her."

Cam went into the women's room.

Eric stood by the door to the men's room and waited.

Men went in and came out of the men's room. Then Eric decided he had to go. Just after Eric went into the men's room, Cam came out of the women's room.

Cam hadn't found Karen, and now she couldn't find Eric. She stood outside the men's room and waited.

When Eric came out, she told him, "Karen is not in there."

Eric wiped his wet hand on the back of his shirt.

"That's no way to dry your hands," Cam said. "There are paper towels in there and an electric hand drier."

"I know. But I thought you might come out and not see me here and worry."

"Hey," Cam said. "Maybe that's what happened with Karen. Her father came out and she wasn't here."

"She was in there," Eric said, and pointed to the women's room.

"Her father thought she was lost. He went to look for her."

"Then, when she did come out," Eric said, "her father was gone."

"We may know what happened to Karen," Cam said. "We may know why she wasn't waiting for her father. But there's still one problem. We didn't find Karen Kramer."

Chapter Four

Cam and Eric went back to the information desk. There were still lots of people waiting there. Mr. Kramer had moved up. He was now in the middle of the line.

"There you are," Mr. Kramer said to Cam and Eric. "Where's Karen?"

"We didn't find her."

"I'm really worried. I need them to make that announcement."

"I'm worried, too. I need to make my flight," the old woman just ahead in the line said. "I'm going to Seattle. But they have so many gates. I don't know where to go."

"The gate number is on your boarding pass," Mr. Kramer told her. "It's gate eighteen."

"Thank you," the woman said, and hurried off.

"My mother lives in Seattle," Mr. Kramer said. "That's where Karen and I are going."

There was another announcement:

Flight two eighty-eight from Denver now arriving at gate sixteen.

"We think we know what happened to her," Eric said. "We think we know why she didn't wait for you."

Eric told Mr. Kramer that when he came out of the men's room, Karen must have been in the women's room.

"Then it's my fault. I should have just waited there."

People at the front of the line had their questions answered and walked off. Mr. Kramer was slowly moving closer to the information desk.

Mr. Kramer shook his head and said, "Before, I didn't know why she wasn't waiting for me. Now I know what might have happened, but it doesn't help. I still don't have Karen."

There was another announcement:

Karen Kramer, please go to the information desk. Your father is waiting there for you.

"Did you hear that?" Cam said.

"Hear what?" Eric and Mr. Kramer asked.

"They just called for Karen to come here. My dad must have had them make the announcement."

"I didn't hear it," Mr. Kramer said. "This place is so noisy, and there are so many announcements."

Eric said, "Maybe Karen heard it. If she did, she's probably on her way here."

"I hope so," Mr. Kramer said.

Mr. Jansen joined Cam, Eric, and Mr. Kramer.

"Let's go," he said. "I'm sure Karen heard the announcement. She should be here soon."

"But I'm next," Mr. Kramer said.

"Yes, you are," Mr. Jansen told him. "But you're waiting to ask them to make an announcement and they already made it. Now your daughter may be coming here looking for you. We don't want to miss her."

They all went to a small waiting area near the information desk. They stood there and looked for Karen.

Mr. Kramer looked at his watch again.

"It's getting late," he said. "You've been very helpful, but you don't have to wait with me. You must have a plane to catch."

"Oh, no," Mr. Jansen said. "We're not going anywhere. We came to pick up my friend Max."

Mr. Jansen took out his cell phone.

"I forgot all about Max. He must be wondering where we are. I have to call him."

Mr. Jansen pushed the buttons on his phone.

He waited.

"Max isn't answering."

He pushed the buttons again.

"He's still not answering. What happened to Spaghetti Max?"

Chapter Five

Cam, Eric, Mr. Jansen, and Mr. Kramer watched as many people walked by the information desk.

Mr. Jansen said, "Now we're looking for two people: Karen and Spaghetti Max."

"Hey! There's a girl who's about five," Eric said, and pointed.

Cam said, "She's not wearing an avocado shirt."

Mr. Jansen said, "And she's holding her mother's hand."

"She's not Karen," Mr. Kramer told Eric.

"Yeah," Eric said. "I guess I knew that. I'm just so anxious to solve this mystery."

Cam, Eric, Mr. Jansen, and Mr. Kramer stood there a while longer.

"We don't all need to be here," Cam told her father and Mr. Kramer. "We're all watching the same people walk by. While you stay here, Eric and I can go looking for Karen."

Eric said, "We'll also look for a man who's really skinny."

"Stay together," Cam's father said.

As they walked off, Cam told Eric, "I don't like to just stand around. I like to do things."

Cam and Eric walked toward the men's room. They walked past many of the shops in the building.

Then they reached the security checkpoint. Beyond it were the gates. They couldn't go any farther without a boarding pass.

"Where could she be?" Cam asked. "She knows she's lost. Why isn't she looking for her father?"

"And where is Spaghetti Max?" Eric asked.

They looked at the people waiting by

the checkpoint. Those near the front of the line emptied their pockets into a plastic bin. They put their jackets, hats, and shoes in another bin. Then they put the bins on a wide moving belt that took them through an X-ray machine. They put their carry-on luggage on the belt, too. Next the people walked through a large arch.

Cam watched a woman with a small child give the security guard a boarding pass. Then they both walked through the arch.

"Did you see that?" Cam asked. "She just gave the guard one pass. Maybe small children don't need one."

Eric said, "I think she gave him two passes."

"Let's find out."

Cam and Eric went to the front of the line.

"Please, wait your turn," the guard said.

"We're not going in there," Cam said and pointed to the gates beyond the arch. "We just have a question. Does a small child need a boarding pass?"

"Everyone needs a pass."

Eric asked him, "Did you see a small girl with red ribbons in her hair and a green shirt?"

"I've seen lots of people. I don't remember them all."

Cam and Eric looked beyond the checkpoint. They looked at the people on their way to the gates. They didn't see Karen.

Cam and Eric walked away from the checkpoint.

"Karen doesn't have a boarding pass," Cam said. "She couldn't have gone to the gate. So where is she?"

"Let's go back," Eric said. "Maybe she heard the announcement and went to the information desk. Maybe now your dad is looking for us."

They started back. Then, as they walked past a newspaper stand, Eric stopped.

"Look," he said. "I see him."

"Who do you see?"

"Spaghetti Max."

Chapter Six

"That man is really skinny," Eric said. "He looks old, like your father. He must be Spaghetti Max. Let's go tell him that your dad is waiting for him by the information desk."

There was another announcement. This time it was very loud.

Flight fifty-one to Phoenix now boarding at gate twelve.

Cam looked up. The announcement was coming from a metal speaker right above her

Flight fifty-one to Phoenix...

and Eric. The speaker was hanging from the ceiling.

> *Flight ninety-two from Dallas now arriving at gate thirty-two.*

Cam turned and looked at the large computer screen with the schedule of the airplanes arriving and leaving the airport. The information about the Phoenix and Dallas flights was on the screen.

"Did you just hear those announcements?" Cam asked Eric.

"What announcements? It's so noisy here."

"That's the problem. Karen Kramer might not even have heard that her father is waiting for her at the information desk."

"What about Spaghetti Max? At least we found him. He's right over there. Why don't we tell him where your dad is waiting?"

"We *think* we found him," Cam said.

The man was looking at the many newspapers in the racks.

Cam and Eric walked toward the thin man.

Eric said, "Hello, Spaghetti Max."

The man kept looking at the newspapers.

Cam said, "Hello, Mr. Miller."

The man took a newspaper off the rack. He took it to the counter and paid for it.

Cam and Eric followed him.

"Excuse me, are you Mr. Max Miller?" Eric asked loudly.

The man turned. "Are you talking to me?"

"Yes. Are you Max Miller?"

"No. I'm not."

"Are you sure?" Eric asked.

The man laughed and shook his head.

"Are you asking me if I'm sure I know who I am?"

"I'm sorry," Eric said. "That was a silly

question. It's just that we're looking for Max Miller and we've never met him."

"Well, good luck with that," the man said, and walked away.

Cam said, "We should stop looking for Spaghetti Max. He has a cell phone and he has our address. If we don't find him, he'll call Dad or he'll take a taxi to my house. We should be looking for Karen Kramer."

"I am," Eric said. "I'm looking for both of them. I'm looking for a tall skinny man and a five-year-old girl wearing an avocado green shirt."

Eric looked at everyone they passed as they walked toward the information desk.

Cam stopped looking at them. Instead she closed her eyes and said, *"Click!"*

She said, *"Click!"* again and kept walking.

"Hey!" Eric said. He pulled Cam toward him. "Watch where you're going. You almost walked into someone."

"I'm trying to remember everything I've

seen since we came to the airport. I must
have seen something that will help us find
Karen Kramer."

Eric took Cam's hand.

"I don't want you to get hurt," Eric said.

"When we came here," Cam said, "we
saw lots of people pulling suitcases. We saw
people standing in front of the computer
screen looking at the airplane schedule.
We saw all those eating places."

"And there was a long line of people standing by the information desk," Eric said. "And there's still a long line."

"*Click!*" Cam said again. "Now I'm looking at all those toy and souvenir shops."

"Open your eyes," Eric said. "There's someone with your Dad and Mr. Kramer."

"Is it Karen?"

"No. It's some man."

Chapter Seven

Mel Kramer hurried to Cam and Eric.

"Did you find Karen?"

"No," Eric told him. "We looked every-where. We even went to the security check by the gates."

"It's my fault," Mr. Kramer said. "I should never have left her alone." He shook his head and slowly walked away.

Mr. Jansen waved to Cam and Eric. Then he walked to them. A tall, heavy man was with him.

"This is my daughter, Jennifer," Mr. Jansen told the man. "And this is her good friend Eric."

"Hello," the man said. "Barry J has told me a lot about both of you. I'm Spaghetti Max."

"You are?" Cam asked.

"Yes," Max Miller said. "And you're the girl with the amazing memory. Don't you have a nickname?"

"Yes. They call me 'Cam.' It's short for 'The Camera.' People call me that because I have a photographic memory."

"People used to call me Spaghetti Max because I was as thin as a strand of spaghetti. And do you know what?"

Cam and Eric shook their heads. They didn't know what.

"I also like to eat spaghetti . . . and pizza and ice cream and lots of other things. So now I'm not so thin."

"Flying makes Max hungry," Mr. Jansen said.

"Most things make me hungry," Max said. "As soon as I got off the plane, I had a sandwich at Sol's Sandwiches. Then I had a strawberry ice cream cone at Polly's Ice Cream Shop."

"Why didn't you answer my dad when he called you?" Cam asked.

"When I got on the airplane, I turned off my cell phone. That's why I didn't hear his call. I finished eating, turned on my phone, and called your dad."

"He told me where he was waiting," Mr. Jansen said. "I found him sitting at Polly's. As soon as I saw him, I knew he was my skinny friend Spaghetti Max."

Mr. Jansen's friend laughed.

"It's been a long time since I've been skinny."

Now Mr. Jansen laughed.

"Sometimes you see what you want to see," he said.

"Sometimes you see what you want to see," Cam repeated slowly.

Then she closed her eyes and said, *"Click!"*

She said, *"Click!"* again.

"That's it!" Cam opened her eyes.

"I just thought of something," she told her father. "Can you and Mr. Miller wait here? Eric and I will be right back."

Cam hurried off. Eric ran to catch up with her.

"What did you think of?" Eric asked. "Do you know where to find Karen?"

Cam and Eric walked quickly past the information desk. They walked toward the snack shops.

"Do you remember what Mr. Kramer told us about Karen? She saw the word *Men* and thought it said *Menu*."

Eric said, "Kids learning to read do that all the time. Even I did that."

"Yes. You see what you want to see. You see a few letters and think you see a word you know."

Cam and Eric were in front of Sol's Sandwich Shop.

"What would you want to see if you were Karen Kramer and you were lost at the airport?"

"I'd want to see my father."

"What else?" Cam asked. "What else would you want to see?"

Eric shook his head. He didn't know.

"If you couldn't find your father, you

would look for the police. Remember? He said Karen knows not to talk to strangers and to ask the police for help."

Cam and Eric were walking toward Polly's Ice Cream Shop.

"Look at that sign. Do you see the P-O-L and the I-C-E? That spells POLICE. Someone who thinks MEN spells MENU might think POLLY'S ICE CREAM spells POLICE."

There was another announcement:

Flight ninety for Seattle now boarding at gate eighteen.

Cam said, "That's the Kramers' flight. We have to hurry and check the ice cream shop. We've got to find Karen."

Chapter Eight

Polly's Ice Cream Shop was crowded. There was a long counter in front. Beneath the counter, under glass, were tubs of ice cream. Above the counter was a large sign listing all the flavors sold at Polly's.

"Hey, look," Eric said. "You can get a bubble-gum ice cream cone or blueberry raspberry swirl."

"We're not here for ice cream," Cam said. "We're here for Karen."

There was a long line of people waiting to buy ice cream. Cam and Eric looked for a five-year-old girl wearing an avocado green shirt.

Karen wasn't in line.

Behind the line were several small round tables.

"Excuse me," Cam and Eric said as they tried to get to the other side of the line.

"Hey," a man shouted at them. "No pushing ahead. Get to the back of the line."

"We're not here for ice cream," Cam told the man. "We're looking for someone."

Cam and Eric got to the other side of the line. They saw people standing and sitting by the tables. At a corner table they saw a small girl. She had red ribbons in her hair and was wearing an avocado green shirt.

Cam said, "Maybe that's her."

"But she's sitting with people," Eric said. "It looks like that girl is with her family."

"Karen! Karen Kramer!" Cam called as she walked toward the table.

The girl looked up.

When Cam reached the table she asked, "Are you Karen Kramer?"

The girl nodded.

"Come with us," Cam said. "We'll take you to your father."

The girl shook her head. She wouldn't go.

"Do you know this girl?" a woman sitting by the table asked. "She seems to be lost. We tried to help her, but she won't talk to us."

The girl's head was down. She wasn't looking at anyone.

"Karen," Cam said. "Come with us. We'll take you to your father."

"I can't talk to strangers," she whispered. "I'm waiting for my daddy or the police."

"That's what she told us," the woman at the table said.

"Come with us," Eric said, "or you'll miss your flight."

Karen Kramer shook her head. She wouldn't go.

"You stay here," Cam told Eric. "I'll get her father."

Cam hurried to the information desk. "I found her," she told Mr. Kramer.

"Where is she?"

"She's at Polly's Ice Cream."

Mr. Kramer, Mr. Jansen, and Spaghetti Max followed Cam to Polly's. Mr. Kramer hurried to his daughter. They hugged.

"I was so worried," he said. "What are you doing here?"

"I was lost," Karen said as she got up from the table. "You told me to go to the police when I'm lost. So I came here. But the police didn't come. I think they're busy."

Mr. Kramer took his daughter's hand. He looked at his watch.

"Let's go," he said. "We have to catch our plane."

He told Cam and Eric, "I should give you two a reward."

"No, you shouldn't," Cam said. "You should hurry to gate eighteen."

Mr. Kramer smiled. "I can't thank you enough for finding Karen," he told them.

Cam, Eric, Mr. Jansen, and Spaghetti Max watched Mr. Kramer and Karen hurry toward the security check by the boarding gates.

"We should go home now," Mr. Jansen said.

"Oh, no," Spaghetti Max told his friend. "That man was right. These children deserve a reward. Let's have some ice cream."

"I know what flavor I want," Eric said. "I want blueberry raspberry swirl."

Cam said, "I want a bubble-gum cone."

Spaghetti Max said, "I'll have a strawberry cone with chocolate sprinkles."

Mr. Jansen looked at the large sign which listed the many flavors of ice cream sold at Polly's. He thought for a few moments. Then he said, "I'll take a dish of vanilla ice cream."

"*Vanilla!*" Max said loudly. "All those choices, and you want vanilla?"

"I like vanilla."

"It's been almost thirty years since I saw you, and you haven't changed," Max said. "You always liked things plain and simple."

"You're right," Mr. Jansen said. "I haven't changed. I still like vanilla ice cream, and I still have the same good friend."

"Are you BFFs?" Eric asked. "Best friend forever?"

"Maybe," Mr. Jansen and Mr. Miller said.

Cam looked at Eric.

Eric looked at Cam.

"That's what we are," Eric said. "We're BFFs. Best friends forever."

A Cam Jansen Memory Game

Take another look at the picture on page 11. Study it. Blink your eyes and say, *"Click!"* Then turn back here and answer the questions at the bottom of the page. Please, first study the picture, *then* look at the questions.

1. How many toy animals are on the table? What are they?

2. Who is pointing at the toy animals?

3. Does Cam have stripes or dots on her shirt?

4. Which toy animal is holding cymbals?

5. Are Cam and Eric the only people in the picture?